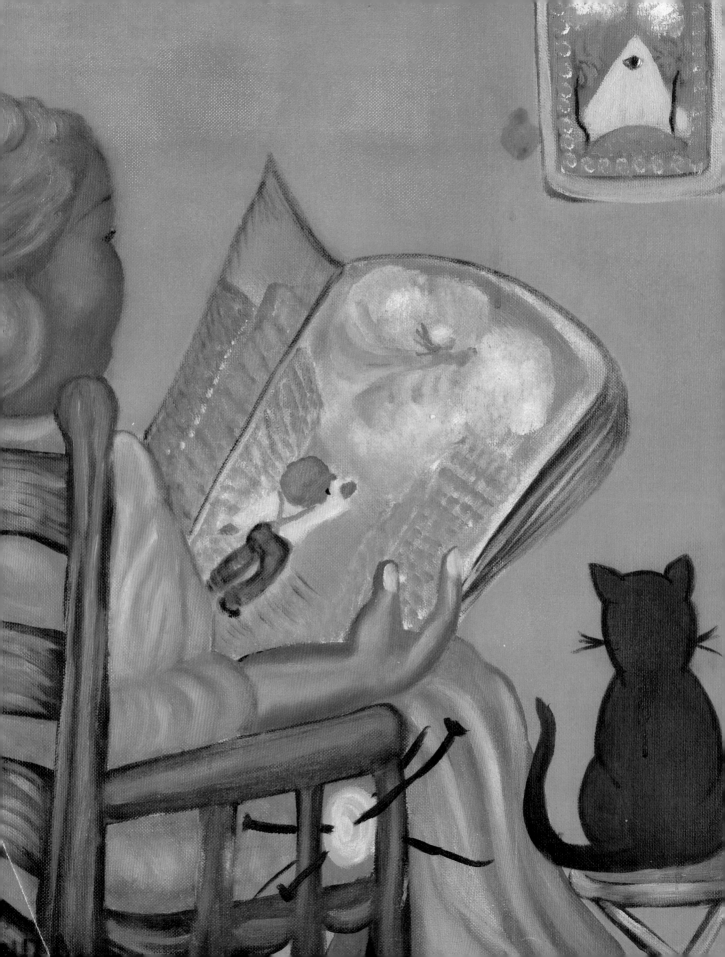

Jamal and the Angel

AN AUNT MARTHA STORY
By Anita Rodriguez

Clarkson Potter/Publishers
New York

It was Monday in the heart of the big city. Aunt Martha had just baked oatmeal cookies for Jerry, Marybelle, Lisa, and Little Mark, who often came to visit her after school.

"Today," said Aunt Martha, "I'm going to tell you a story about a little boy who used to live in this very neighborhood, and about his angel."

"What are angels?"asked Lisa.

"Angels are special beings who are usually invisible," answered Aunt Martha. "Some say they can fly and once in a while they can be seen by people.

"But, children," said Aunt Martha, "let me get on with the story."

Not quite so long ago, in the heart of the big city, the sun was shining brightly on the tall, old buildings.

Jamal walked along thinking about his dream. He was going to be a musician when he grew up and what he wanted most in the world was a guitar.

When he got to his house, he ran up the 83 steps to the apartment where he lived with his mother, his brother, Jesse, his little sister, Joy, and his little puppy, Popo.

Jamal always came straight home from school so that his mother wouldn't worry. He was a good boy.

Jamal started his chores. Everyday, he emptied the trash and helped take care of his baby sister and walked Popo. His mother gave him a 25¢ a week for his allowance. He decided to start saving it for a guitar, though he knew it would take a long time to save up enough.

Jamal asked his mother if he could have a guitar for Christmas.

"Son," his mother said, "you will have to pray about it because right now we do not have enough money."

So every night before he went to sleep, Jamal said
his prayers and asked God to help him get a guitar.
He prayed and prayed all through the months
before Christmas.

It was nearly Christmas and Jamal had saved $3.25. He bought his mother flowers. He made a rattle for his baby sister, Joy, and a sailboat for his brother, Jesse. He was very pleased.

On Christmas morning, he opened his gift. It was a karate suit his mother had made him. He felt proud and happy in his karate suit. But he did not get his guitar.

One night something strange happened.

"Jamal, Jamal!" a voice called out in his bedroom.

Suddenly, a very tall man appeared. His face was radiant and he wore a long robe of rainbow colors.

Jamal was frightened. "Wh-who are you? Where did you come from?" Jamal asked, trembling.

My name is Benjamin," the tall man said in a deep voice. "I am your guardian angel. I am always with you but you usually can't see me. Don't be afraid."

Still frightened, Jamal asked in a shaky voice, "What do you want?"

"Oh, nothing to worry yourself about," answered Benjamin. "I have heard your prayers and I am going to help you."

With that message, the angel disappeared. Jamal had a hard time falling asleep that night, wondering about the angel.

The next day when Jamal went out on the street, he felt the angel with him. He wasn't afraid anymore.

While he was at school, he knew the angel was with him.

One day, when some mean boys stopped him on the street, Jamal just smiled at them and they ran away. Jamal wondered if they had seen the angel.

One afternoon, Jamal walked home on a different
street. Suddenly, he felt a tap on his shoulder. He
stopped and found himself in front of a pawnshop.
There in the window was a beautiful red guitar.
He gazed at it longingly.

An old man came out of the store. "My name is
Manuel," he said. "I know your family. I am looking
for someone to help me out in the afternoons. Will
you ask your mother if you can help me?"

So it was that every day after school Jamal went to help Manuel. He dusted and swept and ran errands. He felt the angel with him as he worked.

Now that Jamal earned extra money he could help his mother and save some for his guitar, too. You see, children, he never gave up on his dream.

One day as Jamal finished up his tasks, the old man said, "Jamal, you have been a big help to me and I want to give you a present."

Manuel brought out a long box.

Jamal opened it and found the beautiful red guitar he had seen in the window.

"Oh, thank you, thank you!" said Jamal. He couldn't find enough thank-yous for the old man . . . and God . . . and the angel, Benjamin.

That evening when Jamal went to say his prayers, the angel was waiting for him.

"Well, Jamal," said Benjamin, "let me see if you can play your new guitar."

So the angel, Benjamin, took out his harp and Jamal took out his guitar and softly plucked the strings. My, what joyous songs they played that night!

This book is dedicated to Suzette, Magic, Lisa, Karl, and Jason.

Published by Clarkson N. Potter, Inc., 201 East 50th Street, New York, New York 10022. Member of the Crown Publishing Group.

CLARKSON N. POTTER, POTTER, and colophon are trademarks of Clarkson N. Potter, Inc.
Manufactured in Hong Kong

Library of Congress Cataloging-in-Publication Data
Rodriguez, Anita
Jamal and the angel/Anita Rodriguez
Summary: Jamal, a little boy from the inner city, gets the guitar he longs for with the help of his guardian angel, Benjamin.
[1. Guitars—Fiction. 2. Angels—Fiction. 3. Afro-Americans—Fiction.] I. Title.
PZ7.R6188Jas 1992
[E]—dc20   92-11636 CIP AC

ISBN 0-517-58601-0
0-517-59115-4 (GLB)

10 9 8 7 6 5 4 3 2 1
First Edition